The dust never settles

Caprice Reader № 3

Cover art by Erik Otto, 2013
www.erikotto.com

Published by Caprice Books
Las Vegas, NV, U.S.A.

For information regarding any of the work in this
book, you may contact the publisher here:
capricebooks@gmail.com

Reply, if any, will be slow.

Insofar as the work in this book expresses or inspires
any opinions, theories, concepts, notions, ideas or
thoughts (deep or otherwise), note that this is a work
of the imagination. Responsibility for conclusions is
the reader's.

Printed on planet Earth.

The dust never settles
Caprice Reader № 3
ISBN 978-0-9849159-0-3

Visit us on the web!
capricebooks.blogspot.com

Do not expect much.

for mike the great

CAPRICE BOOKS

Ingredients:

PAINTING

POETRY

FICTION

ESSAY

MURAL

ILLUSTRATION

Untitled

As I walk swiftly between the four walls, the room grows smaller with every step. I have paced about fondling my cool black lighter for the last decade of hours. An epiphany rises....My hand has refused to release this portable flame for an immeasurable amount of time. If I simply place this on the table, what will my hand have to keep it occupied? What will become of us if we are not distracted in our isolation, my flame and I?

The end of an everyday garden-variety yellow no. 2 pencil catches my eye. It is severely indented from what appear to be teeth marks. What creature could have caused such damage? One might imagine that such a mangling denotes a twinge of stress in the life of the pencil owner. I do not have to imagine or guess that this conclusion is false. Only the art of second-guessing could cause this sort of damage. The creature must have been attempting to free the eraser from the confines of its prison. Incessant rewriting is the cause of the strange disappearance of the soft pink end of the writer's tool. What will I gnaw on in angst now?

Ah! My sweet lady nicotine can cure this anxious feeling. The cherry burns brighter with every drag. How clever my girl is, so inviting and lovely this stick of deception. Every breath crystallized in a mentholated wonderland, I need a drink.

-Avery Ebeneezer Salo

VESPER CHIMES

Crumbling
Edwardian awake
at three I fuse
each hissing into
reaching tours
fires over marshes
where my clay lamp
used to burn
the mansion is of Saturn
its exaltation Mars
nothing flattering
but imperial robes
wishing inkstains
at every leisure
thank the bloodroot
& Cherokee rose
the first of millions
to lick the shores

say hello to my new

necropolis, his voice

is like a plate of rocks

noisy but controlled

when carried

accept the apologies

herewith, I have lost

my place in service

of persuasion

how ahead of the game

how behind the times

a fluent presence

shooting straight up

to collapse!

-Micah Ballard

PROVISIONS

The ingredients
don't know
they're being added
they want us phoned in
loosely smothered
without a cosmos
I lean on my dead pen
the page of cups
reversed
speak plainly snake
before I light you up
our sleep is short
a holy high
of blinking codes
peculiar fares
warring factions
in lieu of that
follow the ash back
I know you want
the classics
but what about
the new miracles?

-Micah Ballard

Comin' or Goin'

"Mom," asked Billy, "Teacher says we come from dust. Is that right?"

"Yes, I think you could say that Billy."

"She also says that when we die, we turn back to dust. Is that right?"

"Sure, Billy. That's right."

"Well then," said Billy triumphantly, "you'd better look under my bed. Someone's either comin' or goin'!"

As the Good Book proclaims, "Dust thou art, and unto dust thou shalt return!"

And the dust never settles.

Every microscopic organism, every animal, every plant, every person that ever lived on earth is still here. The molecules that once provided their form and enabled their function have simply been rearranged.

It really is true!

The disintegrated components of all the plants, animals and people here before us are in the air we breathe, the water we drink, the things we use, the clothes we wear and the dirt on which we walk and in which we grow our food, and, therefore, even in the food we eat. And after our current forms revert to their components, we will join them. How is this possible?

It has to do with the "Law of Conservation of Energy."

This is the law that says the total amount of energy in an isolated system (e.g., the earth, the universe) remains constant. Energy (both chemical and kinetic) can change its location and form within the system but it can neither be created nor destroyed.

It also has to do with the "Law of Conservation of Mass."

Because Einstein's theory of special relativity showed that energy has an equivalent mass, and that mass has an equivalent energy, scientists believe that all particles, both massive, such as protons, and mass-less, such as photons, have energy and mass equivalents.

As with energy, mass can be neither created nor destroyed, although it may be rearranged in space and changed into different equivalents.

It's difficult for us to wrap our minds around the concepts of *eternal* and *eternity*. We can, however, understand that the components of our planet and the universe have been here from the beginning and will all continue to exist as long as the universe exists, however "eternal" that turns out to be. And, since we, as human beings, consist of these same components, we too, component-wise, "have always been and always will be" coeternal with the universe.

Although he made no reference to the laws of conversation of mass/energy, Henry David Thoreau understood the basic concept:

> "How beautifully…[leaves] go to their graves! How gently they lay themselves down and turn to mold! … They that soared so loftily, how contentedly they return to dust again, and are laid low, resigned to die and decay at the foot of the tree, and afford nourishment to new generations of their kind, as well as to flutter on high! They teach us how to die." *(From "Fallen leaves," begun in 1841 and included in Thoreau's essay, Autumnal Tints.)*

Both humans and animals, of course, have more than physical, or molecular components. Central to their nervous systems and thought processes are the chemical synopses that allow cells to communicate with each other to move muscles, stimulate growth, and interpret such external stimuli as temperature, color, sound, taste, motion, pressure, texture, etc.

There are also electrical synapses that use ionic currents to communicate whenever fast response and coordination of timing are crucial, as in escape reflexes.

Central to human beings, of course, is the development of the brain — generally considered to be superior to the brains of all other animals. The human brain contains about 10 billion nerve cells, or neurons. On average, each neuron is connected to other neurons through about 10,000 synapses. The brain's network of neurons forms a massive information processing system.

Like the brains of all animals, human brains learn from experience. They are also very fast, and can even repair themselves if slightly damaged. Most importantly, our human brains support our intelligence and self-awareness, although scientists do not yet know how this works.

There are also immune synapses, which immune cells use to communicate via a peculiar mix of molecules arranged in concentric rings.

But no matter how impressive these complex systems are, all their wonderful components — physical, chemical and electrical — were brought together from materials that have existed since the beginning of the universe and which will continue to exist after our current conglomerate forms cease to function.

The cells of our bodies are constantly regenerating a substance called Adenosine Tri-Phosphate (ATP), using glucose and oxygen and producing carbon dioxide and water.

Tim Dawson, a Fellow of the Royal College of Pathologists, explains that when we die (i.e. our heart beat and breathing stop) our cells continue for a short time to use up stocks of glucose and oxygen and utilize ATP for cell processes before the chemical reaction slows and ceases – maybe several hours after the heart stops, depending on body temperature.

One of these processes keeps muscle fibers sliding over each other. When all the ATP is used up, the muscles of a dead person become stiff, which is known as Rigor Mortis.

ATP also keeps potent digestive enzymes locked up in the cells. When the ATP is used up, these enzymes break out and start digesting the body cells from inside – a process known as Putrefaction. At this point, the protective mechanisms that keep bacteria at bay in the intestines are lost and these invade tissues and begin to breakdown fats, proteins, etc., consuming the energy locked up in them. Eventually, everything is recycled.

Dr. Eram Rizvi, a Senior Lecturer at the School of Physics and Astronomy, Queen Mary University of London, explains the process in simpler terms by saying that the energy we have when we are alive is all in the form of chemical energy – "a bit like a battery." Some of it is also in the form of heat energy, but this is quickly lost as a dead body cools down.

He adds that when we die, most of the energy we had remains as chemical energy of one sort or another when bacteria start to use our bodies as food. If the body is buried, this chemical energy powers the organisms that feed on the body. On the other hand, if the body is cremated, then the chemical energy is turned into heat energy that escapes as hot gases.

Either way you look at it, none of our components are destroyed, just as they were not created specifically for each of us. They simply continue to be rearranged or transformed. And, in keeping with the laws of the conservation of mass/energy, they remain coeternal with the universe!

Whether they want to or not, future

generations of plant, animal and human life will be living with our components in one form or another and absorbing them into their own systems. Perhaps Mary Frye had also realized this when, living in Baltimore in 1932, she wrote the following poem:

"Do not stand at my grave and weep,
I am not there; I do not sleep.
I am a thousand winds that blow,
I am the diamond glints on snow,
I am the sun on ripened grain,
I am the gentle autumn rain.
When you awaken in the
morning's hush
I am the swift uplifting rush
Of quiet birds in circling flight.
I am the soft star-shine at night.
Do not stand at my grave and cry,
I am not there; I did not die."

Perhaps it was also an early realization of this that led to theories of transmigration and reincarnation. And since all our components remain coeternal with the universe, it is scientifically conceivable that the Creator, as a final show of power, could certainly "resurrect" all humankind in the forms they once had.

"But, wait!" you say. "Aren't we more

than conglomerates of living organisms and systems and parasites that live both in and on our bodies? Isn't there a spiritual entity unique to each of us that will also survive our physical conglomerate? What about the human soul?"

Because scientists have yet to know precisely what to look for, they have not been able to devise an instrument to detect the spiritual entity we like to call the soul. Nevertheless, a majority of people, both past and present, believe such an entity exists. They also believe that, through prayer and meditation, spiritual entities can be contacted for help and guidance — the results of which are amply attested in both literature and lore.

It was in an effort to form binding arrangements with such spiritual entities (including with the Unknowable, Inconceivable, All-Powerful Creator and Maintainer of the universe) that people devised religion — from the Latin *religio*, meaning a binding, a tie, or reliance. The pagan Greeks and Romans, and the early Hebrews, structured such binding arrangements between themselves and spiritual entities very legalistically. That is, if they offered X to a spiritual entity and agreed to act in a certain way, then they believed that that spiritual entity was bound to respond with Y. The priest, called a *pontifex* (i.e. "pons," a bridge + "fex." builder), was the official go-between.

If intelligence and self-awareness are, as religions teach, part and parcel of the soul, it may well be that we do indeed have a spiritual component. And because this component seems unique to each of us, resulting from our personal makeup and the way we live our lives, it would seem logical that it, too, would remain coeternal with the universe, even though we have yet to formulate a "Law of Conservation of Spirit."

But that, as they say, is "a whole nuther" discussion.

For now I'll leave you with this albeit religiously lukewarm thought from a letter written by Justice Oliver Wendell Holmes to Sir Frederick Pollock on May 26, 1919:

> "It seems to be probable that the
> only cosmic significance of man is
> that he is part of the cosmos,
> but that seems to me enough."

-Bernard F. Barcio, L.H.D.

Index No. 8

Evolving is for people who are confident

Unraveling is for the rest of us

My abbreviations are uncanny and you
shouldn't

know how I really feel. It does no one

any good. Trying to navigate the shadow of
a circus

or breath in sonic allusion. There's little use

My hands are positioned to orchestrate

And the corners of morning are round in
madness

-Sunnylyn Thibodeaux

Index No. 3

for Sarah Menefee

As the dust settles

there's a machine, unmercied

falling. A glorious array of strangely

shifting takedowns breaking the already

broken. Where a circle starts   light

but revolted. Cornered.   I've been dead

here before but never quite in this variation

Unwound relativity, unalternating rise

All that's left is the shadow of liberty

picking at our pockets. Hollow particle

My voice is the only mortar and my friends

have taken lodging   elsewhere

-Sunnylyn Thibodeaux

Yoga hands
-Francie Taylor

FOR SHAKIR BALOCH (ONE OF THOUSANDS PLUCKED FROM THE STREETS IN THE DAYS AFTER SEPTEMBER 11)

the erupting towers
unleash a fireball
of hatred

rising with the smoke
a cloud of
xenophobic reaction

startling and horrific
as the towers' collapse
it too claims its' innocents

I can hear the shouts
of Shakir Baloch
unemployed doctor
hopeful in New York
looking for work
as a cabbie
(a familiar injustice)

wrestled to the ground by
New York police,
but they are heroes
aren't they?

under arrest with no reason
suspicious appearance
resembles a terrorist maybe
he has…"that look"

taken to detention
no notice given to anyone
24 hour surveillance
arms bound
solitary

his wife in Canada
frantic for weeks
no word from Shakir

how many more
"disappeared"
(a chilling word we've heard before)
how many more
swept from the streets
after September 11

how many more
still detained
hidden away
arms bound
solitary

without charges
without bail

without trial
without anyone
knowing

Shakir Baloch
is home now
still uncertain why

still wondering
how many more
remain hidden

for this list of victims
is not published
their faces are
far too telling

-Jeffrey Shantz

Blanket of Denial

Stop. Stop right there. You think you can escape it? It's no use. Embrace the pain. Embrace it and accept it. There's nothing that can stop them. It covers the land,

blanketing all the past misery. Although you may not admit it now, you know that your life was nothing but a circle of horror, stress, and loss. The time is ticking away. Only a few more minutes until it's all over and we can finally rest. There is no hero to swoop in and save us. You people wrap yourselves in stories and movies and ignorant ideas of farce and fantasy. You think you can deny real life, but there is no stopping it. The dust will never settle. Never. You think the good guys will always win? Do me a favor and get rid of your blanket of denial. This is the end of your story. I pity you all.

-Madeline Daniel
text & illustration

Del and Hilda (1 year later)

Del here. Haven't heard back from Acme about the recording yet. Hilda's party was a big success. Greta took us out for dinner at the hotel where she's staying. She inquired as to why we were still living in a trailer on a pig farm.

I said: Why not? I also told Greta that there was a possibility we might get a call from a recording company shortly and who knows how things could change then.

About a week later I was over at Maynard's. We headed out on a can run. There was a new area that looked promising. We saw a sofa someone had dropped by the side of the road. Need I say more?

Hilda liked the sofa. It was missing a leg. Nothing a couple books didn't fix.

I'm working on my folding guitar. I might try someone other than Acme this time. That's Acme the guitar company, not Acme the recording company. I'm thinking "Guitars Are Us Kids." I was walking by the Amargosa School yesterday and noticed a kid carrying a guitar. He also had on a backpack. Wouldn't it be nice if he could just fold up the guitar and put it in his backpack? It would free up his hands to do other things. I asked him what he thought. He kicked me.

Me and Baby Cakes went for a ride later. We stopped in the Amargosa Animal Shelter. For a second I thought I was looking at Boomer. We took new Boomer to his new home. Later I put the finishing touches on my folding guitar. I had picked up an old guitar somebody had thrown away. Maynard let me use his tools. I got the prototype ready for mailing.

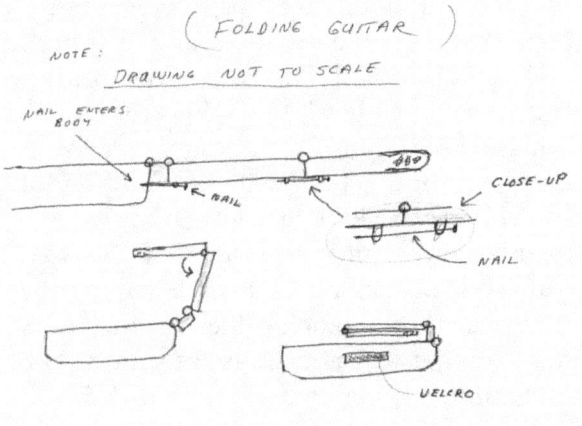

(FOLDING GUITAR)

NOTE :
DRAWING NOT TO SCALE

NAIL ENTERS BODY

NAIL

CLOSE-UP

NAIL

VELCRO

NOTE : VELCRO KEEPS LOOSE STRINGS FROM FLOPPING ALL OVER THE PLACE

NOTE : NAILS PROVIDE NECK SUPPORT WHEN IN PLAYING POSITION

NOTE : IF A NAIL GETS LOST A LONG SKINNY SCREW WILL WORK

Something's come up. Looks like Maynard is thinking of selling the farm. We have been discussing this. He's got a buyer for the pigs. He's going to keep Arnold of course. Maynard says he might just go live with his brother Wilbur for a while. David says he heard there's a shortage of pencils up north, so he might head up there. Maynard was worried about me and Hilda. Nothing to get concerned over yet.

The trip down to Barstow only took a couple hours. I went straight to "Guitars are Us Kids." The manager came out. I said I had something he might be interested in. Maynard had let me borrow an old suitcase he had in the shed. The guitar was inside so the manager didn't know what was coming. I opened it and pulled out the guitar. At first he didn't recognize it. As I unfolded it I could detect a bit of curiosity in his expression. I couldn't unfold it all the way cause one of the bolts got stuck. I went out to the car for a wrench. When I came back the manager was gone. His assistant said he had an unexpected emergency. He left instructions for me to give the folding guitar to the janitor. I wasn't so sure this was a good idea, but was told the janitor was in charge of new products and has been a trusted employee for three months. I asked when production would start. He said he wasn't sure but for me to leave my address and I would be contacted.

Now I'm working on my last guitar-related invention. It's a guitar/shovel combo. I was walking by a construction site and the guys were on a break. One guy was playing a guitar. He said he always carried his guitar around, and played whenever he got a chance. He said the problem was that by the time he got the guitar out of the trunk, break time was almost over. I said I have a possible solution. I said I am a guitar player and inventor. He said: You must be Del Krebs? I said: You are right, sir. He said he'd heard about me. I said: Wouldn't you like to be able to play on a second's notice? He said: Yes I would. I said: What about a shovel adaptable guitar? It would increase your playing time considerably. No need to take it in and out of the car. It would always be available. He seemed excited. I said I was working on a couple variations and would get in touch. I said he could help me market it. He said: What happens if somebody wants to borrow your shovel and isn't a guitar player? I didn't want to give away too many secrets because there were other guys listening. Not to worry, I said. It will be designed in a way that will permit the guitar to be removed. Anyway if the shovel belongs to the construction company you would remove it at the end of the day. Also you might want to do some shoveling at home and the guitar attaches to almost any shovel, except maybe those made in Costa Rica. He said: It might also work with a pick. I said: Good thinking, but let's not get ahead of ourselves.

I got home and Hilda was there. I thought she was supposed to be working. She said: I quit. Boomer misses me when I'm gone and anyway I was really just doing it for the exercise. I said: I dig. Hilda said her boss wasn't going to pay her for the last day since she quit early. He changed his mind though when she threatened to pound him into the floor.

I put the finishing touches on the guitar/shovel combo (the blueprints, not a working model). After seeing the blueprints you're probably going to wonder why I didn't just screw some clamps on the back of the guitar. Wonder no longer. Doing so would make the guitar stick out too much and it might get damaged while in shoveling mode. Also, what if you just want to play the guitar over the weekend without the shovel? The clamps would definitely gouge into you when playing.

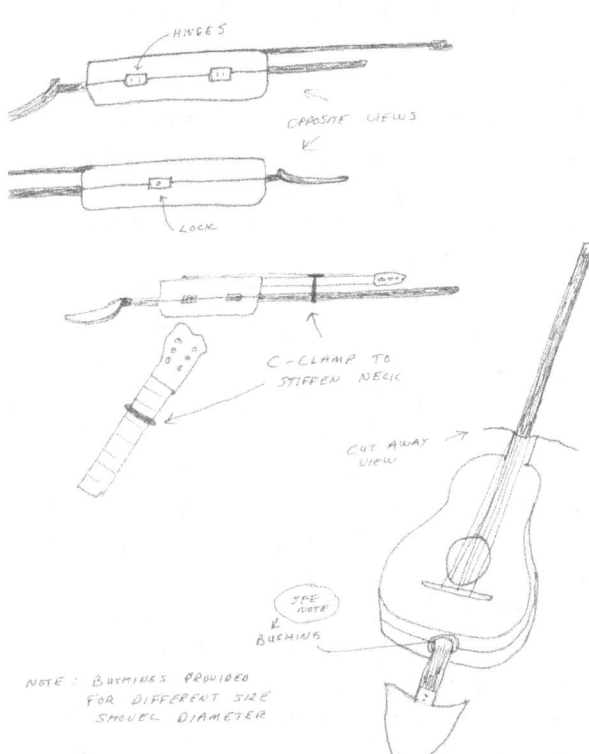

GUITAR/SHOVEL COMBO

HINGES

OPPOSITE VIEWS

LOCK

C-CLAMP TO STIFFEN NECK

CUT AWAY VIEW

SEE NOTE

BUSHING

NOTE: BUSHINGS PROVIDED FOR DIFFERENT SIZE SHOVEL DIAMETER

You might also be thinking: Why not just drill a big hole through the guitar and slide the shovel in it? Won't work. What if the shovel has a handle on the end?

You might also be wondering if the big hole in the guitar would affect the

33

sound. It wouldn't. The guitar being wood and the shovel handle being wood would probably enhance the sound. The sound might even travel up the handle, offering a stereo effect. If the handle is made of some other material, of course the sound will suffer. This is a choice the guitarist must make. As designed, the guitar has more of a custom look and could eventually become a collector's item.

Me and Hilda went for a walk along "Old Potato Road" yesterday. Not much out that way. We did pass Wakimoto's Feed Store. Hilda got a little edgy when she saw the bales of hay. I said: Control yourself Baby Cakes. Boomer did what Boomer always does, on top of a bale. A guy came out and started after Boomer. Hilda went into action. She got there just as he was about to kick Boomer. She blocked the kick. She picked him up by the neck and asked him if he would like to re-consider the kick. He said: Yes and that Boomer was a fine dog.

You might be wondering how me and Hilda met. I was at a bus stop one day. I was doing a little picking while I waited for the bus. Hilda was there. She said she liked my playing. I told her I was headed to the Acme Guitar Company to promote my guitar/rifle case combo. She said she worked at Acme and said she could help me. I wonder what happened to the blueprints after Hilda left Acme. I asked Hilda once. She said when she was arrested they were on top of her cleaning cart. Guess we'll have to wait for hunting season to see if my plans were stolen.

Rare portrait of Del and Hilda Taken at the "Logandale State Fair"

Well, Maynard has a buyer for the farm. David headed up North this morning. We had a going away party for him. He played his new harmonica that he got from Wayne Raney in Clint Texas.

Maynard says he has a month to

move. He said the buyers didn't want our trailer so we could have it. Maynard says he has a friend who has some land next to the cemetery. We're welcomed to it. Electricity might be a problem.

And guess what? I had a funny feeling about this. A folding guitar has surfaced in Mexico. Looks like my suspicions about how things were handled in Barstow are true. The janitor was behind it. Seems he took the guitar down to Mexicali. His brother, who sells guitars, then gave it to a friend who has a taco stand and makes guitars on the side. Not much I can do, being as how it's in Mexico. Actually I don't really care one way or the other.

Got a letter from Greta the other day. Hilda had mentioned that we'd be moving. Greta seems to think we should buy a house. Greta lives in Montecito. It's somewhere on the coast of California. We were planning on taking a road trip, maybe pick up a few gigs. I guess we could head up that way.

The trip to Montecito was uneventful, except for one thing. About 10 miles from Montecito the engine fell out of the Rambler. I guess it's time to replace her.

Greta sent a car to pick us up. Hilda and Greta acted as if they hadn't seen each other in a hundred years. Boomer liked the place. You could tell he was nervous when we got to the house. He unloaded on the front steps. The butler took immediate action. I was impressed. He didn't talk much. Said his name was Waldo. Somebody fixed lunch. We ate on the patio. You could see the ocean.

We stayed in the guesthouse. Next morning I was ready to head back to Amargosa Valley. Greta would have none of it. She had a proposition for us. At dinner we met her husband, Willard. He's some kind of lawyer. From what I could gather, he specialized in banking/financial stuff. I wasn't particularly fond of the food. Actually I don't even know what it was. A fried baloney sandwich would have been better. I didn't let on though. Would have been bad manners.

Willard said he spends a lot of time flying around the world. Work related stuff. Anyway the proposition was that there was a house for sale down the way and we should buy it. Reason being the sisters would be close. I would also have all the room I needed for inventing and guitar playing. I might even have my own recording studio.

I decided me and Boomer would head back. Hilda would visit a little longer. I asked Greta where a good place was to start hitchhiking. She said anywhere was fine if I wanted to end up in jail. She said she had a two-year-old Cadillac they were going to donate to charity. She said I could have it seeing as how I refused to spend any money or become a part of normal society. Seemed a little sarcastic to me. However I accepted the car. I said I might need some money for expenses on the way back, and asked where a good place to set up and play would be. Again the ending up in jail bit. She stormed out of the room. Willard was listening in. He gave me fifty dollars.

Me and Boomer left early the next morning.

We pulled up to the farm. Maynard was still there. He said he had decided to stay in Amargosa Valley. He said he was looking at 20 acres for sale a bit farther out of town.

We drove out to take a look. There were a couple ranches nearby, but nothing else. Perfect. Maynard said he had the down payment. And it had a small abandoned house on it.

I had an idea. I asked Maynard: What

if we were to go in together? I explained how Greta was pushing for us to buy a house and join normal society. I don't like it up there. I don't like it one bit. But I should get a better place for Hilda. And I think Hilda likes it down here better. So our problem might be solved. I'd have to run it by Hilda, of course. We shook on it. Now I could tell Greta I was joining normal society.

I called Hilda. Just my luck, Greta answered the phone. I told her about the land I was buying. A silence, then Hilda came on. I told her about the land. She approved.

I said we could live in the abandoned house while we built a new one. Maynard would use the trailer. Greta came back on. She said although she thought I was in the process of losing my mind, she never saw Hilda so happy. Therefore she is sending an architect down and also a real estate agent.

Me and Maynard stayed in the big house since he had another week before he had to move. The next morning we moved the trailer to the new land. The real estate agent showed up the next day.

Me and Maynard decided to keep the down payment for extra spending money. I would pay cash for the land.

Hilda came back the next day. We met with the architect. He looked at the abandoned house and made plans to rebuild it as a guesthouse. All the doors would be shaped like guitars, and there would be a recording studio. Also a weight room for Baby Cakes.

We're putting up a big sign at the entrance. The D&H Ranch. Maynard is staying. He'll be the ranch foreman.

I think I forgot to mention. Hilda is expecting. Probably why Greta is lightening up a little.

Greta approved the plans. All except for the guitar shaped doors. She does have a point. Be hard for people to go through the door without squatting down.

She approved the bronze statue of Johnny Cash, as long as we put it in the back yard.

Three years later

Hilda had twins. Boy and girl. Their
names are Biff and Iris. We spend a lot of
time in the studio. We're putting together
an album of Donna Fargo's greatest hits.
My inventing has slowed down. Maynard
did ask me to put together something. It's a
way to have the chickens lay the eggs
directly into the egg carton.

Heard from David the other day. He's
playing harmonica with a traveling band.
He said he'd stop by some day when he's in
this area.

Hilda almost got arrested. She beat up
the meter reader. He made some remark
about the Johnny Cash statue. Everything's
okay though. Willard got the charges
dropped.

Pa's monthly checks are history. The
oil wells went dry and he spent all the
money he had investing in a company that
made shoestrings out of recycled plastic
bags. Doesn't matter. I was using the money
to pay kids to take guitar lessons from me.
Ma said she hasn't heard from him in a
couple years. She's working as a waitress in
a small café. She tried to get some money

out of me. Hilda put the Kibosh on that idea. I had told her once about how they had treated Boomer. She didn't like it one bit.

I got some horses for the kids. Maynard will take care of them.

Gotta run. Iris is trying to lift a rock over her head.

-Frank Morelli

remember the dust

3.
worlds collide like a coincidence
on the expressway to nowhere

in my mind's eye time is waiting to occur
unaware of infinity's presence already
engaging in full contact,
no one's looking in traffic
while my own destination races
at speeds undetermined by quanta
and final exits

to contact experiences my Spirit
already dreamt into creation
individually
if I held them out
to offer them to you

you would not be able to grasp them
like gold-dust diggings slipping
through the filters of fingers,
does it mean they have any less
significance,
serve no purpose?

I look into the filter of my own mirror

to see if I can peel through it
like rearview cracked too used to its own
ways,
but there is no spoon to point,
no direction to bend -- they are all already
bent,
so I leap out of skin
to spin out of control
to reveal what I do not know

{must have forgotten to hold on}
to remind me this out-of-body experience
must be where I come from,
I am mostly empty space any way
(so they say),
so what holds me together to remain this
way
when I descend?

as I crashland&burn
I return into craters
that signify resurrection
after destruction,
where people are now
rebuilding neo cities
out of sin cities
to re-begin processes
how they see fit selectively
with festivities

-- phoenix's claws leave ridges
where We once stood originally,
took our chances
built upon contributions from history...

remember the dust
(like Lenny remembered Sammy Jankis;
does he still to this day
turn to photographs burnt?)

no longer apparent in the flesh,
buried beneath fingertips,
nails are tombstones
which no two are alike

epitaph reads:
here lies so & so
remembered for such & such

born the same day he died.
Rest in power,
See You around the corner.

0.
I scrape through screens
planted in stands before me
as if to make a difference
like elections,
while subtle white walls play projections
and keep You and I padded for separation,

disassembled
and unaware of the haze and distortions --
there are far too many
illusions at hand
mask is plaster
shaped into my face,
glass, the encasement
for choices to be made freely,
lenses bend into the horizon
falling as curtains with no applause,

and all I see are the pointed lights...
I release lives from my hands held skyhigh
if I can even recall them
that change like the seasons
to leave me behind
like leaves camouflaged in the wind,
unable to speak until between transitions

do I trust what is in front of me
... distractions aside,
hidden in labels
and smiles?

master of illusion
winks with guile,
ego pursues to become
the illusionist that outlives me...

3.
We must all contribute to something
common
because We all participate in the same
program
replaying in front of us without
interruption,

We must all be in on the act
under contract without acknowledgment,
making cameos in each other's sets,
pre-scripted

as extras rolling dices,
blowing luck on wheels
spinning one click at a time,
swimming in pools that drain
where we don't look

how much is proof without approval…
We create art
but it's participation to be labeled,
who then does the credit roll for,
who stays seated till the reels end
and the breakdown begins?

cleanup to setup next stage
or leave the rubble where it remains…
images stagger on flammable surfaces
held up against the light

that slit through hands,
melt on tongues,
fill lungs that take deep rises
as repetitions turn into patterns,
I watch my step
and drop further
down rabbit hole tunnelings

(as if pill to take
to forget or remember)
and wake up on the other side
where Life was a dream
I now see dissolving like filmstrip
clippings

my eyes, too, now widely open
{or wiggling with lids still in r.e.m.}
among vacant rows and empty seating,
filled with visions I won't be able to recall
exactly,

which is more real?

-Prince Alvior

Fine Art Backgrounds - Gary, IN (*originally in color*) Dan Thompson, FAB Crew fabcrew.com

Detail at Subsurface - Indianapolis, IN *(originally in color)* Dan Thompson, FAB Crew fabcrew.com

The Dust Never Settles

FROM peter_j@bmf.corp
TO Franky1657@ewol.com
2-12-39 10:12 AM
Re: Ieee!

Ieee, Bubby! I'm sorry sorry sorry! You can't believe how much trouble it's been to get the satellite set up. The wind never stops. Now that I can finally send communications, I have too much to say to fit it in a single email. So I'll just start here: I miss you terribly. I miss everyone, but especially you. You can't imagine how isolating the past few weeks have been. Even Adam had the company of the beasts. I don't have an animal or a tree or even a blade of grass to keep me company. But there is much to enjoy (geologically speaking) and work to be done, so no more complaining. I volunteered after all.

If there is one aspect of this whole experience so far I would want to share with you it would be the uncanny beauty of Martian nightfall. The sunset is so familiar and yet so strange. This is what makes new races of men, Frank. Subtle differences in experience. I'm becoming a Martian, Frank. The first Martian.

I'm working on something poetic to say to the press but the languages of Earth are useless to me. So I have set out to construct a Martian language, however it flows from my dry, red lips. "Ieee" is the first Martian word. It means, "Hello," "You are loved," and "I cherish this moment," all at the same time.

Ieee, Frank! Hit me back.
Peter
Western Hemisphere, Mars

FROM Franky1657@ewol.com
TO peter_j@bmf.corp
2-17-39 11:24 AM
Re: Ieee!

Ahhhh! Finally! I was afraid your lander had crashed. They told me it hadn't but I was beginning to think they were hiding something.

Of course I have to point out the obvious: You have invented a greeting first before any other words, even though you are the only resident of that world. Wishful thinking?

Your voice is wonderful to read. How long until we can actually talk? Seems to me it's the same technology as email. But what do I know? Just another stupid sociology professor. And why did it take four days for your email to get to my inbox? I thought stuff moved quicker in space.

Your observations gave me a huge smile, and made me miss you all the more. You're becoming so philosophical lately. I love it! I showed your email to Jeffa, the new concierge. He says he wished he could have met you.

Ieee back at'cha, Love!
Frank
Sent from my iPhone 26

FROM peter_j@bmf.corp
TO Franky1657@ewol.com
2-22-39 4:16 PM
Re: Ieee!

Dear, dear Frank,
Leave it to a Stanford Man to hyper-analyze everything. There is a method to my etymological madness. Don't you read the papers? A second settler is preparing to join me in claiming the red planet. A female specimen. (So you don't have to worry about that!) She's a paleontologist, Frank! Another ologist to talk about all these rocks with! I'm told she'll have an upgraded

Dome-acile™ from the one I brought up. It's got an air conditioner. I admit I'm jealous.

Tell the new concierge your husband says hi. Jeffa is it? Sounds nice.

Peter
Western Hemisphere, Mars

FROM Franky1657@ewol.com
TO peter_j@bmf.corp
2-28-39 09:01 AM
Re: lax

Jeffa is just a friend. Not even a friend. He's just a nice guy who works in our building. What am I supposed to do, stop talking to other people just because you decided to live on another planet for two years? Christ. Anyway, he watches me and Barker on our midnight walks. You want me to be safe, don't you? By the way, your paleontologist friend did an interview in the Village Voice last week. She said she isn't just coming up there to do science. She also happens to be a pro skateboarder. Two-time X-Game silver medalist. She intends to open up the first Martian skateboard supply shop: "Lifted." Whoever's paying for all this apparently thinks that'll be the perfect way for people to get around up there. No gas or batteries required.

Have you thought up any more words? I could use one that means lonely, horny, depressed and desperate for human touch.

Frank
Sent from my iPhone 26

FROM peter_j@bmf.corp
TO Franky1657@ewol.com
3-4-39 4:16 PM
Re: lonely, horny, etc.

The Martian word for what you're feeling is "Hulff." I'm feeling a little hulff myself, Frank. I'm embarrassed to even mention this, but whoever packed my spaceship actually included one of those masturbation sleeves in with the medical equipment. You know the ones? They look like a Pringles can without the label. Normally I wouldn't want anything to do with a contraption like that, but I'm way past my breaking point, Bubby. I got to the point about a week ago where I actually tried the thing out, but guess what. They forgot the lube. And I can barely work up enough saliva to keep my throat from closing up. I can't get a break. Just as well. Wouldn't be the same without you anyway. Stay strong, Bubby. Two months down, 22 to go. No one said monogamy was easy. Seriously, no one has ever said that.

Peter
Western Hemisphere, Mars

FROM Franky1657@ewol.com
TO peter_j@bmf.corp
3-10-39 09:13 AM
Re: Hulff

Thanks, Love, I needed a laugh! The thought of you with that Pringles can or whatever it is. ROTFLOL! You're right, we're being tested. We've just got to stay focused and remember our vows. By the way, someone at BMF Corp left me a message. They said I could send a care package along for you on the next supply drone. Its months away, but I thought I'd prepare. What's the one thing you need? (Besides lube!)
Frank
Sent from my iPhone 26

FROM peter_j@bmf.corp
TO Franky1657@ewol.com
3-15-39 6:44 AM
Re: The one thing I need...

You! Send you! Second best would be a

back massager. Or better yet one of those massage chairs like they have at the airport at the phone recharging station. I've been moving these big rocks around trying to make a giant X on the ground so the skateboarding paleontologist will be able to spot my settlement from the air. I know she has the coordinates, but machines don't work for shit up here. Dust gets in everything. I realize there's no guarantee she'll want to be my neighbor at all. It's a big planet. But hopefully, being a businesswoman, she'll recognize my value as a potential customer. Why should we both be alone? I never mastered skateboarding on Earth, but I anticipate the lower gravitational pull of Mars will offer me an advantage in the Martian version of the sport. Booyah! (I think that's the word.)

I love you Frank, and trust you completely.
Peter
Western Hemisphere, Mars

FROM Franky1657@ewol.com
TO peter_j@bmf.corp
3-19-39 10:38 PM
Re: The one thing I need…

Peter,
Why do you sign off with that Western

Hemisphere, Mars business? Feels like you're showing off. Do you think I don't realize where you are? And you never answered why it takes so long for these emails to go back and forth. I feel like somebody's holding up the transmissions on purpose. Are we being monitored?

I did some research. Do you have any cornstarch? If so, and you can extract a little water from the permafrost, you can easily make your own lube. Mix 4 Tsp cornstarch with one cup of water, boil, reduce to a simmer then stir to get the lumps out. Store it in an airtight container or it'll spoil. If you don't have cornstarch, potato starch will work just as well. Meanwhile, I'm reading a book about asceticism Jeffa gave me. I'll send you a copy. We need to adopt a monk-like perspective. Jeffa says he identifies as an Asexual. Sounds like a solution to me!
Best regards,
Frank
Sent from my iPhone 26

FROM peter_j@bmf.corp
TO Franky1657@ewol.com
3-24-39 7:15 AM
Re: ally?

Best regards? Seriously Frank? Where's the

love? Listen, I appreciate that you need companionship, but do you think it's appropriate to be talking with the concierge about our sex life? I've never even met this person. And yes we're being monitored. What did you think? You knew this was a corporate gig. BMF monitors everything. And no, I don't have any cornstarch. Or potato starch. Or laundry starch. No starch of any kind. Thanks for the tip. Actually, seriously, thanks. I think I owe you an apology, Bubby. I guess I'm the one who started talking about sex with that masturbation sleeve business. I never even thought about all the people at BMF Corp reading everything we write. Jeez. Sorry. These are difficult times. But pay attention, I have something important to tell you.

My sponsor at BMF Corp told me that the paleontologist's skateboard shop is also going to be carrying a full line of Martian swimming apparel. There are plans for a lodge up here with a giant pool and a mud spa and everything. It'll be a regular tourist trap in no time! They're sending sample swimsuits up for atmospheric testing then there's talk of bringing up a crew of professional swimsuit models for a photo shoot next summer! So guess what! I sent your headshot over to BMF! I have always said you should model, haven't I? Well this is your chance! Imagine watching the Martian evenings descend together. It would be so, I don't know, romantic I guess. That word sounds ineffective. I need a Martian word, a word that means perfect calm, sensuality, togetherness and inner peace all at the same time. How about Oomfa? Yes, oomfa. I want to experience oomfa with you, Frank. It would be nice to experience it with anyone of course. But especially you :)

Love and oomfa, Frank, and hopefully soon an end to hulff.

Peter

Western Hemisphere, Mars

FROM peter_j@bmf.corp
TO Franky1657@ewol.com
4-3-39 8:19 AM
Re: Hello?

Frank, are you there? Is everything okay? You didn't respond to my last email. I hope I didn't offend you. Listen, they make me put that Western Hemisphere, Mars line at the bottom of my emails, BMF does. I have no idea why. Hit me back, Love. I miss you!

Peter

Western Hemisphere, Mars

FROM Franky1657@ewol.com
TO peter_j@bmf.corp
4-8-39 10:38 PM
Re: Oomfa

Sorry, Peter. Oomfa. It sounds so lovely. Oomfa. Oomfa!

Listen, I've started drinking again. I don't want to hide anything from you. I'm not proud of it. I just don't know what else to do. I haven't been going out, just staying at home. And Barker is fine. Jeffa has been watching him for the past two nights. I was afraid I would forget to feed the poor thing. I'm taking a few weeks off work. I told them it was a medical leave. I just need to work through this, that's all. I hope you understand. I feel like I'm going insane.

Dreaming of oomfa,
Your Frank
Sent from my iPhone 26

FROM peter_j@bmf.corp
TO Franky1657@ewol.com
4-14-39 5:22 AM
Re: Barker

You sent our dog to a stranger's house? Frank, darling, what the fuck? I'm devastated to hear you are drinking again. I would love to hold you and tell you everything is going to be okay, but yeah, hello, I'm on another planet. You need to be stronger, Frank. You need to be a warrior, for me. For us. Think of your blessings. You have Barker. You have the dog-sitting, ascetic concierge. You have Carol and everyone at work. What do I have? I would give anything just to be joined for five minutes by one of those frantic centipedes I used to stomp in the bathroom back on Idaho Street. I'll never stomp another bug, Frank, that's for sure. I'll never intentionally kill another creature of any sort under any circumstances, other than self-defense. I understand the value of life. All life. Any creature is a potential companion. Even an enemy would be welcome here. Even that awful Paige!

How's this for perspective: I got down on my knees last night and prayed to God as a last resort to stop me from befriending the rocks. Imagine me, praying to God. (Not that I'm unreligious, but He's just so dramatic.) Anyway, I prayed for a ghost to visit me. No rocket ship needed. God's answer so far has been no.
Peter
Western Hemisphere, Mars

FROM peter_j@bmf.corp
TO Franky1657@ewol.com
4-21-39 5:22 AM
Re: Helloooo?

Frank, what's going on? It's been a week.
I'm worried about you. Don't shut me out. I
made up another Martian word. "Aooo." It
means "Bye for now," and "I'll see you in
my dreams," and "Take Care of Yourself,"
and "I love you," all at the same time.
Aooo, Frank.
Peter
Western Hemisphere, Mars

FROM Franky1657@ewol.com
TO peter_j@bmf.corp
4-26-39 1:52 AM
Re: I am so sorry.

Peter my love, I have a confession to make.
A horrible, horrible confession. I am so
sorry. I have been unfaithful, Love. I beg
you, please do not hate me. It was the
alcohol, and the loneliness. And it was once,
Peter. Only once. It wasn't with a stranger.
It was someone I trust. It was just a horrible,
desperate, lonely, awful mistake. I'm yours
forever, Love. I am so sorry. Aooo?
Frank
Sent from my iPhone 26

FROM peter_j@bmf.corp
TO Franky1657@ewol.com
5-2-39 6:42 AM
Re: Sorry?

Frank,
I am crushed. I haven't slept since reading your confession. I have shed the first Martian tears. It was Jeffa wasn't it? Dammit, Frank!
Peter
Western Hemisphere, Mars

FROM Franky1657@ewol.com
TO peter_j@bmf.corp
5-7-39 12:16 AM
Re: Sorry?

It wasn't Jeffa. I told you, Jeffa is asexual. Listen. It was Russell. He and Elliot broke up. We went out for drinks to commiserate. It just happened. We lost control. I'm so very lonely, Peter, and so very, very sorry. Please believe me, I love you and need you now more than ever. Somehow I hope you can find a way to forgive me for this. And Russell is sorry, too. I know it's hard to hear that. He's back with Elliot already. It was all just a big mistake. I'm sorry I hurt you.
Frank
Sent from my iPhone 26

FROM peter_j@bmf.corp
TO Franky1657@ewol.com
5-13-39 8:58 AM
Re: Forgiveness

Frank,

Grace is real. We are flawed creatures. I forgive you. I need you to take ownership of your choices. You're blaming the alcohol and the loneliness. When we give ourselves the option to fail, we fail. You made this mistake, Frank. You have to stop drinking and stop making excuses. I love you. In fact I wish I had your brain up here with me right now. BMF Corp dumped a huge responsibility on me this week. I feel like I'm about to snap. They told me to start working on a Martian Constitution. They said to start by establishing a basic legal standard for the colony, blah blah blah. I told them I don't have any experience in this kind of thing. I'm totally stressed out about it! They say they're interested in observing what sort of society we Martians are going to make for ourselves. They don't want to interfere. A wise decision if you ask me. They don't know what it's like up here. Nobody knows! Except me. And soon the skateboarding paleontologist will know. Then the bikini models. Speaking of which, I seriously think you should get some body shots taken, Frank. Show your calves. Put them up on one of those amateur model sites. I mean I put in a good word for you, but a little cheesecake wouldn't hurt your cause. Anyway, here are the laws I have made up so far: The laws of the first Martian colony:

Law #1: No whining.
Law #2: No littering.
Law #3: No murdering people.
Law #4: Cell phones in designated areas only. (Knew you'd like that one!)
Law #5: Feel free to kill yourself. Just do it in a way that doesn't make a mess.

I would say that I'm married to the first three, but when the bikini models get here, I might have to re-evaluate the cell phone thing, which means law number five could take on new importance. Come to think of it, I may want to reconsider law number three. Imagine, a bunch of bratty, self-obsessed bubbleheads lying around half-naked breaking laws one and two. Say goodbye to Eden! This is how Adam must have felt when Eve arrived.

Aooo, Frank. Remember, love is a feeling. Fidelity is a choice.

Peter
Western Hemisphere, Mars

FROM Franky1657@ewol.com
TO peter_j@bmf.corp
5-18-39 8:43 PM
Re: Grace

Dear Sweet Husband, how can I ever repay you for your understanding? Jeffa says to tell you you are the most beautiful creature, spiritually speaking, that he has ever heard of. I read him the line from your last email about grace. He shed a tear. I don't deserve you, Love. I have not had a drink in four days. I did have a funny thought last night. When the bikini models arrive, they'll work for the skateboarding paleontologist, right? The population will increase, but even though you were there first, she'll be the one in charge. How are you going to keep control? Something to think about.

Awaiting the next Martian word with baited Earthly breath,

Frank

PS: I got a new phone. Free upgrade!

Sent from my iPhone 27

FROM peter_j@bmf.corp
TO Franky1657@ewol.com
5-23-39 8:58 AM
Re: Control

Dearest Frank, leave it to a sociologist to cut

through the bull. Here I am facing my own obliteration and I'm behaving as though it's a remedy for all my problems. More settlers isn't a remedy. More settlers is a disease!

As a precaution, I got rid of my giant X and plan instead to abscond to a high peak when this skateboarding paleontologist arrives so I can keep an eye on her for a while and make sure she's the right kind of people. A good Martian! She could be a cannibal for all I know. Or a Satanist! I wouldn't know a devilish skateboarding paleontological bikini cult from the regular kind of skateboarding paleontological bikini cult. Now that I think about it, I don't even have an alarm system. Anybody who wanted to could march right into my Dome-acile™ and do God-knows-what to me. I've forgotten what it was like on Earth, Frank. Like a distant love affair, the farther into the past my relationship with humanity recedes, the less I remember the bad and the more I romanticize what little good there was.

Thanks for looking out. I'm proud of you for kicking the booze. I know we can survive this. Stay strong.

Peter

Western Hemisphere, Mars

FROM Franky1657@ewol.com
TO peter_j@bmf.corp
5-27-39 6:02 PM
Re: Control

Peter my love I'm afraid you might have misunderstood. It seems like you're overreacting. I was just worried about you up there, alone, vulnerable. I'm sure the new settlers will be fine people. Just make sure you assert yourself, that's all.
Love forever,
Frank
Sent from my iPhone 27

FROM peter_j@bmf.corp
TO Franky1657@ewol.com
6-1-39 5:11 AM
Re: Ha!

Fine people? Seriously? Is there any such thing? I was giddy as an elf over the arrival of more humans. But were the Cherokee better off with more humans? How about the bald eagle? Or the manatee? Or the white tiger? How did the wooly mammoth fair against more humans?

And to think I was actually praising this fiend for introducing capitalism to Martianity! Solitude has poisoned my mind. I still want you to send me some pictures of you in your swimming suit, Bubby. But steer clear of this skateboarding paleontologist and her bikini-clad army of death. I'll have a greeting for her when she arrives, but it won't be ieee! It'll be a sentro-bomb! I'll knock her little space ship right out of the sky then get to work directly on Martian Immigration Laws.

Hear that Suzy, and all the rest of you reading this at BMF Corp? Only the right type of person is going to be allowed on Mars from now on.

I'll see you in 19 months, Bubby. Your soul mate and fearless defender of the Martian way,
Peter
Western Hemisphere, Mars

FROM Franky1657@ewol.com
TO peter_j@bmf.corp
6-7-39 9:05 AM
Re: Ha!

Peter, you have to calm down. You're being paranoid. It's the isolation. Tell me you've come to your senses. I was only kidding when I brought the question up about who's going to be in charge. There's nothing to be in charge of, Peter. The new settlers are coming to help you. They're your colleagues, Peter. You're not a killer. For God's sake, you're a geologist!

Frank
Sent from my iPhone 27

FROM auto_reply@BMF.corp
TO Franky1657@ewol.com
6-7-39 9:06 AM
Re: mailer daemon

This is an automated reply. Delivery to peter_j@bmf.corp has failed permanently. There is no such address. Do not reply to this message. Error number 367hr394g67.

-Phillip Barcio

THE CAROUSEL

The winters in Michigan are cold. My older sister Melissa (we called her Maggie) used to come home late from her job as a cocktail waitress, run into my twin sister's and my bedroom and tickle us with her ice cold hands. She was 14 years older than us and we loved it. We would stay up long after we'd gone to bed and await that cold tickle. She always smelled a little bit like cigarette smoke and fried food. Most restaurants in Michigan tended to.

I wanted to be a waitress ever since those days. I'd watch her come home with her short black apron all stained up and filled with cash. Occasionally she and her other waitress friends would baby-sit us during the days. They had a system down: In the afternoon, they laid out by Gina's pool and rubbed baby oil on their bodies and drank Big Gulps of unsweetened Iced Tea. They read magazines and didn't care if we splashed them when jumping into the pool because it cooled them down. At night, they worked at Coscerelli's, the local Italian restaurant where they made cash money in tips and a lot of it (at least it seemed like that to me because when we would go through the Burger King drive-through we could order whatever we wanted).

When I turned 14, I got my first "watiressing" job at my aunt's Bingo Hall on the south side of Lansing. It was called The Carousel. It was connected to a halfway home for women and seemed to host many people who were in transition.

The name, Carousel, was confusing because the Bingo Hall was really just a big L-shaped room with long tables and bad lighting. Also, the idea of a halfway home being a resting point between somewhere in the past and somewhere in the future; visually it seems more like a long line instead of a circus ride that goes round and round. Or does it?

My twin sister and I worked there at the concession stand, which was really just a cart with snacks and drinks that we would push around the big room. The short part of the "L" was for non-smokers, reserving the largest part for smokers. There really wasn't anything stopping smoke from spilling into the "non-smoking" area and everyone there smoked.

I hadn't realized that Bingo was such a superstitious game until I worked there. Patrons would arrive an hour early or more to set up their altars. Beanie Babies, candles, tiny family photographs, crucifixes, and other figurines would be carefully and intentionally placed around the Bingo Cards in front of the player. I also didn't realize how many bingo cards people could or would play at a time. 10, 20, it seemed to be an infinite possibility. Some people used the tiny clear plastic markers to place on the numbers but most people used the "dabbers." They looked like small circular deodorant sticks that had different color ink inside. When a number-letter combo was called out that was on one (or many) of the cards, they would dab it. That way there was no risk of the marker sliding off and leading to what was called a *false* bingo.

It wasn't the dabbers or even the figurines that made me realize how precious this game was. It was the yelling. At me. I would be walking slowly and cautiously down each aisle watching, listening for someone to call out for a bag of Frito Lays or a caffeine-free Diet Coke, or a Dew. My large, empty, plastic peanut container lined with dimes and nickels, jingling.

Like a flight attended I was careful of limbs, and moved quietly past those who had fallen asleep. I was even more careful of the prized altarpieces. God forbid I knock over Jesus and the Lamb mid call. But it wasn't enough. The listening wasn't enough. Not for me, not for them. They needed to also *see* the small TV's mounted in the corners of the room that displayed the called numbers, current and past. Inevitably, no matter where I stood, how fast or slow I moved, I was in the way, blocking someone's view, and that was not okay. And so the roar, from the side of the mouth, through the dangling Virginia Slim 150 (the long ones): "Move it!" or, "You're in the way!" or, "JESUSSSS, I can't SEE!" This would always invoke anxiety in me, and fear and a desperate attempt to locate the person I was blocking so I could make way, but it always led to knocking tables and limbs and it always resulted in blocking someone else's view and it always made me miss the call, "DEEEWW!"

In my mother's blue Astro van on the ride home each night, we would count our nickels and dimes and change our clothes to hang in the garage--they always smelled like cigarettes and fried food.

-Terra Haywood

Contributors:

Prince Alvior co-hosts the Human Experience open mic every Monday at The Beat on Fremont Street in Las Vegas. Poetry and the relationship with words has been the greatest tool to help him understand himself and cultivate creativity. His work has appeared on angryasianman.com and in the *ViVa Vegas Poetry Anthology*. He has participated in the *Undeniables* online workshop and in poetry events around Las Vegas. He says lets change our world together…We are all one…do better…evolve…Love~ dreamsoflucidity.wordpress.com

Micah Ballard lives in San Francisco. He is the author of over a dozen books of poetry, including the collections *Waifs and Strays* (City Lights Books, 2011), *Parish Krewes* (Bootstrap Productions, 2009), and *Evangeline Downs* (Ugly Duckling Presse, 2006). With poet Sunnylyn Thibodeaux he co-edits Auguste Press and Lew Gallery Editions. Currently, he works for the MFA in Writing Program at USF. www.poetryfoundation.org/bio/micah-ballard

B. F. Barcio is a retired Classicist who spent years bringing Classical Latin to life both in classrooms and on stage as a 1st Century A.D. Persona Presenter. During his professional career, he wrote hundreds of educational articles and now enjoys writing short, true stories about his camping and travel adventures. He is the author of the memoir *That's Not the Way I Remember It* and the speculative fiction novel *Raising Jesus, The Early Years*.

Phillip Barcio is a writer and artist who lives in Vegas with his wife and a dog who wears a sweater. For fun, Phillip secretly slips his self-published books onto the shelves of bookstores and libraries. He is the author of the book *Television Hates Itself* (Caprice, 2012) and creator of *Bagazine*, a zine featuring his original poetry, fiction and cartoon art written on a paper bag from Trader Joe's. bagazine.tumblr.com

Madeline Daniel was born in 2001 in Evanston, IL. She has lived there ever since with her mother, father, and little sister. Madeline grew up writing. Even before she could spell, she would take a pen and fill in pieces of lined paper with squiggly lines. She has a love for strange, dark and creepy things and likes learning new words to use in her writing. Her life-long dream is to have a book published.

Terra Haywood is a graduate of the SFAI School of Film. She is a multifaceted, multitasking, double Gemini, identical twin queer, natural born storyteller, performer and master of confession. Nothing is left unsaid. She works in San Francisco as an Art Director and Property Master and professional Dog Walker. In every down moment she is simultaneously working on a book of short stories, a feature length screenplay and a one-person show. Her short-term goal is to stretch more.

Frank Morelli served in the U.S. Navy and now lives in Las Vegas with his wife Candy. Frank is the brother of Caprice Reader #1 contributor Mike Morelli. He lays down sounds on his Les Paul guitar, enjoys relaxing to the sounds of jazz guitarist Johnny Smith and has had many professions, including diamond appraiser. Frank is an inspiration to his family and continues to write his unique brand of fiction.

Erik Otto is a native of the SF Bay area and has worked professionally in the arts for over 10 years. From street corners to distinguished galleries, Otto presents his work on a variety of levels, including installations, theater sets, retail storefronts, and independent film sets. Utilizing a growing list of mediums and reclaimed materials, Otto creates work that is both expressive and conceptual that finds resolution in capturing the moment where beauty meets chaos. www.erikotto.com

Avery Ebeneezer Salo was raised as a savage, living in caves and underground huts. Upon turning 13, she was sucked through a porthole of the damned and cursed to be a muse for all of mankind for eternity. Reclusive and coarsely annoyed with societal ways of the human race, she creates a new love from the remains of souls that she collects through charismatic and psychic vampiric means.

Jeffrey Shantz is a poet, artist, videographer, and activist. His books include *Commonist Tendencies: Mutual Aid Beyond Communism* (Punctum, 2013) and *Against All Authority: Anarchism and the Literary Imagination* (Imprint, 2012). While living in Toronto he hosted two community radio programs for almost a decade. He lives in Surrey, B.C. (Metro Vancouver).

Francie Taylor lives in Fishers, Indiana, and had no idea she could sketch hands till about five minutes ago.

Sunnylyn Thibodeaux is the author of *Palm to Pine* and *As Water Sounds* (Bootstrap), *88 Haiku for Lorca* (Push Press), *Room Service Calls* (Lew Gallery Editions), *Universal Fall Precautions* (Well Greased Press) and *Against What Light* (forthcoming from Ypolita). She lives in San Francisco and has had poems appear in *Amerarcana, Back Room Live, The c_L Newsletter, Death and Life of American Cities, Dusie, The Emerald Tablet, Lit, Poems by Sunday* and *The Gulf Stream: Poems of the Gulf Coast*.

Dan Thompson is a member of FAB Crew (Fantastic Aerosol Brothers), an Indianapolis-based duo who found their calling as muralists after years of working in relative obscurity. Though Dan and his collaborator, Benjamin Long, both are trained in fine art and commercial design, graffiti remains the driving force behind their creativity. www.fabcrew.com

**Also available from
Caprice Books:**

**Caprice Reader #1:
If it won't reach, stretch**

**Caprice Reader #2:
Powerless Point**

**Television Hates Itself
by Phillip Barcio**

**Buy Caprice Books at
capricebooks.blogspot.com
or LuLu.com**

CAPRICE BOOKS